DISNEP

Anna & Elsa

All Hail the Queen

For Ken & Judy David —E.D.

randomhousekids.com

ISBN 978-0-7364-3284-9 (hardcover) — ISBN 978-0-7364-8216-5 (lib. bdg.)

Printed in the United States of America

10 9 8 7 6 5 4 3 2 1

DISNEP

Anna & Elsa

All Hail the Queen

By Erica David

Illustrated by Bill Robinson

Random House New York

Chapter 1

Queen Elsa of Arendelle looked out one of her castle windows. It was a glorious morning in the kingdom. The sun shone brightly. It danced across the waters of the fjord.

Below, the people of Arendelle were just starting the day. Shopkeepers opened their windows and doors. Fishermen walked to the wharf. Ice harvesters set out for the frozen lake nestled in the mountains.

Elsa was proud of her village and the people in it. They had come to trust her, even though she wasn't like most queens. Most queens couldn't cast spells of ice and snow. Most queens couldn't make a walking, talking snowman. Most queens couldn't accidentally set off an eternal winter, leaving the village completely frozen! Not so long ago, Elsa had been worried that the people of Arendelle wouldn't accept her because of her differences, but to her delight, they had embraced her wholeheartedly.

Elsa stepped back from the window.

The beautiful weather made her long to go outdoors, but she had royal duties to attend to. She turned to her desk. The plans she had been working on for the town's new plumbing system were waiting. The pipes and canals would carry water to every part of the village. But the builders couldn't start without the queen's go-ahead.

Elsa sat down and picked up the plans. Seconds later, the door to her study sprang open. Her younger sister, Anna, bounded into the room. Her eyes were brimming with excitement.

"Do you know what day it is?" Anna asked eagerly.

"Tuesday?" Elsa guessed.

"Today's the day we cross number three off the list!" Anna exclaimed. She hurried over to her sister, unrolling a long scroll of paper. It was Anna's list of Things to Do in Arendelle. She'd been keeping it ever since Elsa became queen. Anna cleared her throat to announce number three.

"Florian's Famous Flangendorfers!" she said.

"Flangen—what?" Elsa asked.

"Flangendorfers. The most delicious dessert in all of Arendelle," Anna explained cheerfully.

Elsa shook her head, puzzled. She'd never heard of a flangendorfer.

"Aren't you excited?" Anna asked. She took Elsa's hand and pulled her to her feet.

"I am, but I have work to do," Elsa replied.

"How can you work on a day like this?" Anna said. She twirled around in the shaft of sunlight shining through the windows. "Come on, Elsa, just one flangendorfer."

Elsa bit her lip as she considered. It was such a beautiful day. One flangendorfer wouldn't hurt. "Okay," she agreed.

Anna whooped with delight. "I love our visits to the village," she said. "There's a whole world out there!"

Anna's excitement was contagious. Elsa couldn't help smiling.

The sisters walked through the palace gates. They strolled along the cobblestone streets of the town.

By now the village shops had opened. The town square was filled with merchants. Some wheeled carts of fruit for sale. Others sold beautiful scarves and jewelry. Many waved to Anna and Elsa.

"Isn't this wonderful?" Anna said. "Just look at all there is to see!"

Elsa noticed a small girl making her way through the crowd. The girl carried a bouquet of fresh flowers. She had two dark braids that bobbed up and down. She skipped happily toward Elsa and Anna.

The little girl held her flowers up to Elsa. Elsa smiled and reached out to take the bouquet. "What's your name?" she asked gently.

"Ingrid," the girl said quietly. Now

that she was face to face with the queen, she seemed nervous. Ingrid lowered her eyes and dropped into a deep curtsy.

"It's okay. Don't be shy," Elsa said. She took the bouquet from the girl's trembling fingers. "Thank you for the flowers."

Ingrid remained absolutely still. She looked like she had no idea what to do.

Anna noticed the girl's confusion and gently raised her from her curtsy. She leaned down to whisper in Ingrid's ear. "She's not as intimidating as she looks," Anna joked, pointing to her sister, who was smiling. Elsa didn't look the least bit intimidating.

Ingrid giggled. She waved timidly to the queen. Elsa waved back.

"Oh, what's that on your dress?" Anna asked Ingrid. She pointed to the child's bright blue pinafore.

Curious, Ingrid glanced down. As soon as she did, Anna playfully tweaked her nose. "Just kidding," she said.

Ingrid laughed and squealed in delight. She seemed to forget her nervousness about meeting the queen. She made another curtsy and darted off into the square.

"How adorable," Anna said, leaning over to sniff the flowers. She plucked a sprig of purple heather from Elsa's bouquet and tucked it behind her ear. Elsa smiled. Anna definitely had a way with people.

The sisters weaved through the crowd of villagers in the square.

"Are you sure you know where you're going?" Elsa asked.

"Of course!" Anna replied. "I've been planning this visit forever!"

"Forever?" Elsa said doubtfully.

"Well, maybe not *forever*," Anna admitted. "But at least since you became queen."

Elsa remembered the day of her coronation. Until then, the castle gates had been shut. None of the villagers had been allowed inside. It was all because Elsa hadn't wanted her powers to hurt anyone. She had thought the only way to keep everyone safe had been to keep them out.

On the day she became queen, though,

the castle gates had been opened wide. Back then, Elsa had been worried about her secret. She had been nervous about meeting the townspeople. Anna, on the other hand, couldn't wait to welcome them.

Now Elsa was relieved that she didn't have to hide her powers anymore. She and Anna could leave the palace any time they liked. But although Elsa was free to explore, new people and places took some getting used to after all those years alone.

Lost in thought, Elsa didn't notice the gruff fisherman in front of her. She accidentally walked into him, knocking his basket of fish onto the cobblestones.

"I'm so sorry," Elsa said.

The fisherman grumbled until he

realized who she was. One look at Elsa and his entire expression changed. "No, I'm sorry, Your Majesty," he said formally.

"Please, it was my fault," Elsa said, smiling. She bent down to gather up the fish.

"No, no! I'll take care of that," the fisherman insisted. He bowed deeply and waved the queen aside.

Elsa hesitated. She didn't want the villagers to treat her differently just because she was the queen. She wanted to help.

Anna had been watching the whole scene. She tapped the fisherman on the shoulder.

"Hey, she's not that kind of queen,"

Anna whispered conspiratorially.

"What kind of queen is that?" the fisherman asked.

"The off-with-his-head kind," Anna replied. "She's the kind who really wants to pick up the fish. I think you should let her do it."

The fisherman looked from Anna to Elsa and back to Anna again. "Are you sure?" he said.

"I'm sure. In fact, the *princess* insists," Anna said, pointing to herself.

The fisherman relaxed. A broad smile spread across his face. "Well, if the *princess* insists," he said. He moved aside and let Elsa help him collect his fish. In no time, they'd placed all of the shiny silver trout in the basket.

The fisherman thanked Elsa and Anna for their help. He disappeared into the crowd with his fish.

"How do you do that?" Elsa asked.

"Do what?" Anna said.

"He was worried I'd be angry, but you

knew just what to say," Elsa explained.

"I don't know," Anna said, shrugging. "It's not magic. I just talked to him. I guess I'm a talker."

"I talked to him, too," Elsa pointed out.

"Yes, but you're very . . . queenly," Anna said, grinning. She held up her hand and waved stiffly to the crowd to demonstrate.

"I don't wave like that," Elsa said, laughing. "You make me look like some kind of ice princess."

"Well, aren't you?" Anna teased gently.

"I prefer snow queen," Elsa said lightheartedly. "*You're* the princess."

Anna laughed. The sisters linked arms and crossed the square.

"We're almost there," Anna said.

Florian's Famous Flangendorfers was just down the road. Elsa could already smell the sweet pastries.

Just then, her ears pricked up. A band of village musicians was playing at the edge of the square. The townspeople had gathered to listen. They clapped and swayed to the music.

Elsa and Anna were charmed by the bubbly melody. They walked closer to the band, clapping and snapping along. Elsa drew several coins from her purse. She dropped them into a nearby jar for the musicians.

The musicians recognized Elsa at once. They stopped playing and bowed deeply to the queen. Then they picked up their instruments again. They played a slow, dignified song. It was Arendelle's royal anthem.

Elsa tried her best to clap along, but the song was too slow. It sounded nothing like the cheerful song the band had been playing moments before. The villagers began to fidget. Arendelle's royal anthem wasn't just slow—it was also long.

Suddenly, Anna hitched up her skirts. She kicked up her heels and started to dance. The musicians noticed and played faster. They wanted to keep up with Anna's sprightly steps. Elsa laughed and danced along with Anna. The anthem had never sounded so good!

Soon the villagers joined the dancing

queen and her sister. Everyone moved happily in time to the music. Elsa and Anna danced across the cobblestones all the way to Florian's Famous Flangendorfers.

Chapter 2

Florian's Famous Flangendorfers was more than just a bakery—it was a dessert lover's dream. From the outside, it looked like a gingerbread house. The roof seemed to be made of gumdrops. The front door was painted in a red-and-white peppermint swirl. Elsa had never seen anything like it.

The shop itself looked good enough to eat.

Inside, the bakery was bright and airy. Beautiful glass display cabinets lined the walls. One cabinet was full of gooey toffees and sticky taffies. Another displayed row after row of chocolate bonbons.

Florian's candies looked delicious, but he was really known for his pastries. The buttery croissants, creamy cream puffs, sugary krumkake, and heavenly cakes were kept on the bakery counter at the rear of the shop.

Elsa and Anna drifted toward the counter. They were pulled in by the mouthwatering scent of freshly baked pies.

"Ahem!" said a voice. Elsa and Anna looked up from the pastries. A tall, thin man stood before them. He had a long, narrow face and wore a crisp white chef's coat. A black beret sat on top of his head.

The man swept forward to greet them. "My queen, allow me to introduce myself," he said. "Chef Florian, at your service."

Chef Florian bowed and kissed the back of Elsa's hand. She jumped in surprise. Elsa hadn't expected Florian's dramatic manner. She gave Anna a look that said *This flangendorfer better be good.* Anna smiled sheepishly. She shook hands with Chef Florian but pulled away before he could kiss her hand, too.

Chef Florian didn't seem to notice. He simply snapped his fingers. At the sound, two assistant bakers came from the back of the shop. They carried a fancy table and two chairs. The bakers set the table and chairs down between Anna and Elsa.

"Please, sit," Florian said. He snapped again and another assistant appeared. She held a large platter covered with a shiny silver dome.

Elsa glanced at the huge dome. Her eyes caught Anna's across the table. She leaned forward and whispered, "Anna, what's a flangendorfer again?"

Anna shrugged. "I don't know," she whispered back. "But I hear they're delicious!"

Elsa hoped her sister was right. From the size of the platter, it looked like they had a lot of flangendorfer ahead of them.

"May I present to you the finest dessert in all of Arendelle!" Chef Florian exclaimed. He removed the silver dome with a flourish.

On the platter sat two towering pastries. Each flangendorfer was made of five layers stacked on top of each other. The bottom and top layers were light, flaky pastry. The middle layers were made of fruit, chocolate, and cream. The whole dessert was drizzled with honey. Then it was dusted with powdered sugar.

Elsa gasped, amazed. She picked up her spoon. One bite was all it took to convince her. *Chef Florian is a genius!* Elsa could tell that Anna had the same thought. Here

23

was everything she loved, all in one dessert!

The bakery grew quiet. The only sound was the clattering of spoons against plates. When the sisters finished eating, they relaxed in their seats. Their bellies were quite full. They smiled contentedly.

"Who wants seconds?" Chef Florian asked.

"That was wonderful," Elsa said. "But I don't think I could eat another bite."

Anna opened her mouth to agree. But it wasn't words that came out. Instead, she gave a long, loud belch.

Chef Florian was stunned. He clearly hadn't been expecting that—especially from a princess.

"Anna!" Elsa said, embarrassed.

Anna shrugged apologetically. "Excuse me," she said.

Then Florian began to chuckle. It started quietly at first. But the sound grew until it was a full-fledged laugh.

"That's the best compliment a chef can

get," he said to Anna. "Come, I'll show you the secrets of the flangendorfer."

*

Florian led Elsa and Anna through a curtain behind the bakery counter. On the other side was an enormous kitchen. The kitchen was a blur of activity. Florian's assistants ran back and forth in a swirl of flour dust. They rolled dough, melted chocolate, and piped icing onto delicious treats.

"My family has been making flangendorfers for years," Florian said proudly. "The dessert was invented by my great-great-great-great-great-uncle a long time ago."

"How did he come up with it?" Elsa asked.

"An excellent question!" Florian said. "But the answer is a mystery. Some say he got the recipe from the trolls."

Elsa remembered the trolls. They knew a great deal of magic. But she'd never thought of them as pastry people.

"I think he just put all the best sweet stuff together and—*bam!*—flangendorfer!" Anna said.

"I wouldn't be surprised," Florian replied. "Great-Uncle Klaus loved to eat."

The pastry chef took the sisters over to a nearby table. In the middle was a large mound of dough. Florian divided the dough in half, giving one part to Elsa and the other to Anna.

"This is our special flangendorfer dough," he explained. "I will teach you how to roll it flat."

Anna pushed up her sleeves confidently. She'd baked cookies in the palace kitchens. "Piece of cake," she said breezily.

Florian shot her a warning look. When it came to baking, he was all business.

"Er, flangendorfer, I meant. Piece of flangendorfer," Anna said seriously. She stood up straight.

Florian turned his attention to the dough. "First you must remember to be very quiet," he whispered.

"Quiet? Why?" Anna blurted out.

"Shhhhh!" Florian hissed. "The dough, she is very sensitive."

"She?" Elsa asked. Anna looked at her sister and smothered a giggle.

"Yes. She. The dough is like a fiery princess. You must not make her angry," he explained. "You must speak gently to her . . . with your fingers."

Florian wiggled his flour-covered fingers in the air. He curled one hand into a fist and punched the dough flat.

"That doesn't look very gentle," Anna whispered to Elsa. Elsa did her best not to laugh, but Anna was making it difficult.

Instead, Elsa focused on Florian's instructions. She punched her dough and pressed it flat with her fingertips. The finicky pastry chef inspected her work.

When he was satisfied, he handed her a rolling pin.

Anna's dough was giving her trouble. It stuck to her fingers in a gluey ball. Luckily, Florian didn't notice. He stepped away to check on a batch of cream puffs.

"I think she's angry with me," Anna said softly.

"Who?" Elsa whispered.

"The fiery princess dough!" Anna replied. "She's stuck to my fingers!" Anna shook her hands desperately. But the dough didn't budge.

"Maybe you should apologize to her," Elsa teased.

"What?" Anna laughed.

"Shhhhh!" Elsa replied. "You heard

Chef Florian. He told us to whisper."

Anna sighed in frustration. She wiped one sticky hand against the front of her dress, but that only made things worse. "Now *I'm* stuck!" she whispered to Elsa, trying to tug her hand away from the dough.

Elsa calmly scooped some extra flour into her hands. She sprinkled the flour onto Anna's dough, hoping to make it less sticky.

Unfortunately, the flour tickled Anna's nose. *"ACHOO!"* A gust of flour dust rose into the air when she sneezed. It settled in her hair and on her eyelashes like a fine coating of snow.

Anna reached for a towel to wipe her

face but accidentally backed into a shelf of pots. The shelf toppled, sending pots and pans clattering to the ground with a loud *crash*!

One pot fell into a giant bowl of batter being mixed by an assistant. A big blob splashed out of the bowl, sailed across the kitchen, and landed right on top of the lantern. The flame went out.

Chef Florian peered angrily through the dark. He spotted Anna at the center of the commotion. Anna grinned guiltily. In the silence that followed, she nervously licked the dough from her fingers.

Florian huffed and folded his arms across his chest. Anna tried to opened her mouth to apologize, but again no words came out. "Mmmph!" Anna mumbled urgently. "MMMPH!"

All the chefs and assistants stared at Anna, dumbfounded. Then Elsa realized— Anna had eaten so much dough, her lips were stuck together!

That night, Anna was sitting on the end of Elsa's bed in her pajamas. Her list of Things to Do in Arendelle was spread out on her lap. "I can't wait for number four tomorrow!" she exclaimed.

"Wasn't number three enough?" Elsa asked wearily.

"So I made a little mess in Chef Florian's kitchen," Anna said with a shrug.

"Everything turned out okay in the end."

Elsa laughed. Her sister was right. Somehow everything *had* turned out okay. Even though Anna had brought the whole kitchen to a halt, Chef Florian couldn't stay angry at her. He had laughed so hard that she was immediately back in his good graces. It was true. Anna definitely had a way with people.

It was something Elsa admired about her sister. Elsa wondered if she would ever have that kind of relationship with her subjects—without the mess, she hoped!

Chapter 3

The next afternoon, three visitors arrived in the palace courtyard. They were an unusual trio. First there was Sven, a shaggy, playful reindeer. Then there was Kristoff, an ice harvester who had been raised by trolls. Finally, there was Olaf.

Olaf was a snowman who loved

sunshine and warm hugs. Also, Olaf could talk! In fact, he was talking right now. "I can't wait to get to the lake!" he said. Olaf waved his tiny twig arms in delight.

"Slow down, there," said Kristoff. "We can't leave without Anna and Elsa." Kristoff had promised everyone a tour of the frozen lake high in the mountains. It was number four on Anna's adventure list.

"We're here!" Elsa called. She and Anna walked into the courtyard. They waved happily to Kristoff, Olaf, and Sven. Sven snorted contentedly in his bridle, pulling Kristoff and Olaf in the cart closer to the sisters.

Anna patted Sven's muzzle. The

reindeer nuzzled her gently until he found what he was looking for. In the pocket of Anna's dress was a big, juicy carrot. Sven chomped the carrot with pleasure. Carrots were his favorite treat.

Next it was Elsa's turn to greet the reindeer. She scratched him softly between the antlers. Sven nosed through her pockets but was ultimately disappointed. The queen's pockets were empty! The reindeer snorted his disapproval.

"Hey, not everyone has to bring you carrots, buddy," Kristoff said from his perch in the front of the cart.

Sven turned away from him with his nose in the air.

"Don't mind him," Kristoff said to

Elsa. "Somebody woke up on the wrong side of the barn this morning."

"I didn't!" Olaf offered helpfully.

"I know. I was talking about Mr. Cranky Caribou," Kristoff replied, pointing to Sven.

"Mr. Caribou?" Olaf asked, confused. "I don't think I've met him."

"Of course you've met him!" Kristoff said.

"It's okay, Olaf," Anna interrupted. "You'll meet him someday." She liked to play along with Olaf.

Kristoff jumped down and helped Elsa and Anna into the cart. Then he took his place in the driver's seat. Moments later, they were on their way.

The journey to the frozen lake was a

familiar one for Sven. He and Kristoff had been going there since they were little. They had worked side by side with the ice harvesters for a long time.

Sven climbed higher and higher until they reached the lake. It was surrounded by snow-capped mountains. The frozen water glowed a bright shade of pale blue. A group of hardy men and women worked on the icy surface.

"This is where the magic happens," Kristoff said proudly. He introduced Elsa, Anna, and Olaf to his fellow ice harvesters. The workers were honored to meet the queen, the princess, and the snowman. They bowed deeply and welcomed them.

"Everyone here works together,"

Kristoff explained. The ice harvesters split up into small groups. The first group cut the frozen surface with long saws. They carved blocks of ice from the lake.

Elsa watched, fascinated. The ice harvesters were part of Arendelle's history. They'd been supplying the village with ice for hundreds of years!

Anna saw the rapt expression on her sister's face. "Not bad for number four on the list," Anna whispered to her. Elsa smiled in return. She was thrilled.

Together, they followed Kristoff over to the next group of workers. The men stood over the newly cut block of ice. The ice blocks bobbed up and down on the freezing surface. The harvesters used sturdy tongs to bring the blocks out of the water.

"Can I try?" Anna asked.

"I don't know. The ice is very heavy," Kristoff said dramatically. "Allow me."

Kristoff flexed his muscles, showing off. He fixed his tongs to a block of ice. "Now, what I'm about to do here requires years of training," he said. "Oh, and it doesn't hurt to be strong and robust."

Elsa and Anna rolled their eyes. They knew Kristoff was trying to impress them.

Kristoff lifted the tongs and placed them on the ice block. He heaved his weight toward the block. It bobbed in the water but didn't pop out like it was supposed to. Kristoff laughed nervously and glanced at the sisters.

"I don't think that's how it's supposed to work," Elsa whispered to Anna. Anna laughed.

After several more failed tries, Kristoff finally got the ice block to bob awkwardly out of the water and onto the frozen surface. "And that is how we harvest ice," he said.

Anna took the tongs from Kristoff and walked over to the next block of ice. She easily bobbed it down, so that it popped up and slid onto the surface beside Olaf.

Kristoff's mouth dropped open in surprise. "No way," he said.

"Maybe you should practice more," Elsa told him. She patted Anna on the back.

Olaf stared at the large cube of ice

beside him. It seemed to sparkle with a light all its own. The ice block was almost as big as he was.

"Hey, we have a lot in common, don't we?" Olaf asked the ice. "I'm handsome, you're handsome. I like warm hugs, you like warm hugs. . . . It's like we're family."

Before Elsa knew it, Olaf was pushing the block of ice toward her.

"Elsa! Elsa, look!" he cried excitedly. "It's my cousin!"

Elsa smiled at Olaf. It was sweet, the way he liked every creature he met—even a block of ice that couldn't move. For a moment, Elsa wondered whether she might be able to bring the ice block to life as a real cousin for Olaf. But she didn't need to. Olaf already loved his ice-block cousin just the way it was.

"Cousins are great, aren't they? They're just like . . . like sisters," said Olaf, gazing at Anna.

"Sisters are great, Olaf, and so are cousins," Anna said, "but you have another family, too."

"Oh. I do?" Olaf asked, puzzled.

"You do," Elsa answered. "You have us."

"Oh, yeah!" Olaf said. Now he seemed even happier.

Olaf scrambled to keep up with Kristoff, leaving the ice block behind. The mountain man led them to the final group of harvesters.

"Once the ice comes out of the lake, we load it onto sleds," Kristoff explained. "Then we take the ice into town to sell it."

Elsa watched the harvesters carry ice blocks on their shoulders. They brought them to the sleds waiting on the ice and carefully loaded each one. Everyone worked together, just as Kristoff had said.

"Seeing these blocks together gives me a happy feeling!" Olaf declared. "They're a family, just like us. They even get to ride to town together!"

Olaf looked over his shoulder to see the block of ice he'd left behind. It was all alone. "We forgot one!" he cried. "He has to go to town with his family!"

Elsa watched Olaf race back to the lonely ice block. He pushed it across the frozen lake to the sleds piled high with ice. Olaf tried to lift the block, but his twig arms weren't strong enough!

Elsa hurried over to help the snowman. They each took one side and started to lift. Elsa could move the block a little, but Olaf's side stayed firmly on the lake's surface. The big block slid around as they tried to lift it. Then Anna and Kristoff joined them, and each lifted a corner. At last, with everyone's help, the ice block was settled onto the sled. Olaf waved his twig arms in victory.

Just then, the frozen lake beneath the sled creaked loudly. Large cracks split the surface under the runners. With the extra block of ice, the sled was too heavy!

"Quick, run!" Kristoff yelled.

Everyone hurried away from the sleds. They reached the banks of the lake just in time. The cracks in the ice widened and a huge hole appeared. Three sleds sank into the water, leaving the ice blocks floating on the surface.

Chapter 4

The ice harvesters were a tall, burly group of men and women. They were known for their strength. They were also known for singing songs while they worked. For the most part, they were pleasant people. But they didn't look so pleasant now.

"Olaf was only trying to help," Anna said. "We all were."

The ice harvesters grumbled. Their mouths were turned down into frowns.

"Don't worry, I can fix it!" Olaf said happily. "I'm an ice man, too."

"Technically, you're a *snow*man," Anna pointed out.

Elsa thought about the fisherman she'd met the day before. She'd been so happy when he had let her help save his catch. "You know, Olaf might be on to something," she said. "What if we help restore the harvest?"

"Yes! I can help restore the harvest!" Olaf exclaimed. "How do I do that?" he whispered to Elsa.

Elsa took Olaf by the hand and led him to the leader of the ice harvesters. "We're going to join the team," she explained.

"I've always wanted to be on a team!" Olaf said.

The foreman wasn't sure about Olaf. The snowman was very small compared to the rest of the workers. And Elsa and Anna had very little experience harvesting ice. But for his queen, he was willing to give it a try.

The ice harvesters carefully pulled the remaining sleds back onto the lake. They would have to start all over again, cutting new blocks of ice. Olaf scampered after them, trying to keep up on his stocky, snowy legs. Soon the ice harvesters picked a spot to begin again. They took out their long saws and began to carve the ice.

Kristoff, Anna, and Elsa followed their lead.

Olaf struggled to lift his saw. The blade was long and heavy. It was covered in sharp metal teeth that seemed to frown. "Cheer up, Mr. Saw," Olaf said.

Seconds later, he wedged the tip of the saw into the ice. Olaf looked very proud of himself. Now all he had to do was cut.

Olaf leaned against the handle and pushed as hard as he could, but the saw blade didn't budge. He hopped up and down and pressed with all his might. Still, nothing happened.

Kristoff noticed Olaf struggling and offered to help. He took Olaf's saw by the handle and pushed.

But Olaf must have wedged the saw into the ice at a strange angle. Instead of slicing through the ice, the saw blade bent double. Stunned, Kristoff let go. The saw snapped back with a loud *TWANG,* accidentally smacking Olaf in his carrot nose.

"Sorry," Kristoff said. But Olaf only giggled. He didn't seem to feel any pain.

"Maybe carving isn't your specialty," Elsa said. She gently led Olaf to the group of harvesters lifting ice blocks from the lake. Kristoff followed and handed the snowman a pair of tongs.

Olaf stumbled under the weight of the tongs, but at least they were lighter than the saw. He gazed at the newly cut blocks of ice floating on the surface of the lake.

"Hello, cousins!" he cried, waving to them. "Don't worry, this will be fun! Just like bobbing for apples!"

Olaf swung his tongs open and held them out with his tiny twig arms. He managed to grasp a large cube of ice. But Elsa knew ice, and ice was slippery. She winced as the tongs slid across the slick surface of the ice block and out of Olaf's hands. They fell into the lake with a splash!

Elsa, Anna, and Kristoff cringed. So far, the plan to restore the harvest was not going very well.

"Listen, why don't you help move the ice?" Elsa suggested. It seemed to be the safest job for Olaf. All he had to do was slide the ice blocks across the lake so that a worker could transfer them to a sled.

Olaf nodded eagerly and flexed his little arms, as he'd seen Kristoff do. He found a block of ice and pushed it across the slippery lake. It looked like a success. There were no heavy tools for him to break or lose. He seemed at one with nature.

From the banks of the lake, Elsa and Anna watched, relieved. Olaf had finally found a way to help. He hopped happily back and forth, sliding one block after another.

As the afternoon wore on, the sun moved out from behind the clouds. Its brilliant rays shone down on the ice harvesters. The thick ice covering the lake was starting to get a little slick. Most of the workers didn't seem to mind—their boots were built to keep them safe, and they were used to walking on slippery ice. Olaf had his personal flurry to keep him cool, but he didn't have boots on his snowy feet.

Anna noticed and tapped Elsa on the shoulder. "Is it just me, or is Olaf . . . slipping?" she asked.

Elsa stopped working and stared at Olaf. Anna was right. Olaf was starting to slide more with every step. Elsa could see that a thin layer of water was forming beneath his feet.

"Olaf!" Elsa called out. She wanted to

tell him to stand still until the workers could help him.

Olaf smiled back at them and waved cheerfully. Then he got right back to work. He didn't seem to understand why she was calling to him. He gave the next ice block a hearty shove. But instead of the ice block sliding away, Olaf started to slide in the other direction.

Elsa and Anna tried to run after him, but Anna slipped on the ice. She grabbed Elsa's arm as she slid toward Olaf.

The three of them crashed into a tall pile of ice, sending the blocks tumbling this way and that. The huge pieces fell down around them. Many cracked and split open against the frozen lake. Olaf was surrounded by big chunks of crunchy ice.

When the frost cleared, the ice harvesters were staring in shock. This was the second time today that their visitors had ruined the harvest.

Elsa looked out at the broken ice spread across the lake. She felt bad. It would take the workers days to make up the harvest, but if she used her powers, she could fix everything in moments. After all, ice was her specialty.

"Maybe I can help," Elsa said. She motioned for everyone to stand back.

Elsa raised her arms and summoned her magical powers. An icy wind swirled around her and ruffled her hair. She extended her hands into the frosty gale and then knelt to touch the surface of the lake.

The lake rumbled at Elsa's touch. The rumbling spread outward from beneath her fingers to the center of the lake. There, the ice began to split apart. But instead of cracking randomly, it split into perfect cubes.

The ice harvesters watched in wonder.

They'd never seen anything like this before. The ice blocks slowly came out of the water as a new surface of ice rose underneath them. It looked as though the ice was moving all by itself—but it was Elsa's magic.

In just a few minutes, the entire day's harvest was saved. The ice blocks were lined up in neat rows on top of the frozen lake. All the workers had to do was load the sleds. Elsa gently lowered her arms.

Anna beamed with pride. Olaf and Kristoff stared at her in admiration. They wore the same smiles as the ice harvesters, who gazed at Elsa, amazed. Her powers were a wonder to see.

"Thank you, Queen Elsa!" the foreman said.

"You're welcome," Elsa replied, nodding graciously. "I'm glad I could help. After all, what are queens for?"

The men bowed before her and then quite unexpectedly lifted her onto their shoulders. Elsa gasped, then grinned. This was fun!

"Three cheers for Queen Elsa!" they shouted heartily. "All hail the Queen!"

Chapter 5

When she woke the next morning, Elsa was still glowing with a sense of accomplishment. She'd saved the ice harvest, and the harvesters were happy. The good memory put a spring in her step as she dressed for the day. Elsa strolled through the halls of the palace, happily humming a tune to herself.

Just outside her study, Anna greeted her breathlessly.

"Ready for number five?" she asked, holding up her adventure list.

"Definitely," Elsa replied. "What's on the agenda?"

"A picnic with some friends I met in the village," Anna explained.

"That sounds wonderful," Elsa said. "Just let me grab my cloak. I think I left it in here."

Elsa opened the door to her study, expecting the usual early-morning quiet. Instead, she was surprised by a gaggle of voices coming from outside.

She turned to Anna for an answer, but

her sister looked as puzzled as she was.

Elsa crossed to the windows and looked out. A huge crowd of people had gathered in the courtyard.

"What is it?" Anna asked, coming up beside her.

"I'm not sure," Elsa said.

The sisters hurried downstairs, on the hunt for answers. They were met by Kai, the butler. He was busy directing a handful of servants.

"Kai, what's going on?" asked Elsa.

"The villagers are here to see you, Your Majesty," the butler explained.

"Why? Is something wrong?" Elsa asked anxiously.

"No, Your Majesty," Kai said,

chuckling. "They're seeking an audience with the queen. They want your help."

Kai led Elsa and Anna down the main corridor. He and the servants were getting the audience chamber ready. The audience chamber was a special room where the villagers could visit with the queen.

Outside the chamber, two footmen stood at the ready. They opened two grand doors as Elsa approached. She walked into the beautiful hall with the high ceilings and took her seat on the throne. Anna followed and stood beside her.

"We'll let the villagers in as soon as you're ready, Your Majesty," Kai said.

"All right," Elsa said. She was nervous and excited all at once. The people of the village were depending on her. She wrung her hands and noticed her sister standing beside the throne.

"I'm sorry, Anna. It looks like I won't be able to go to the picnic today," Elsa apologized.

"That's okay. Maybe we can reschedule," Anna said. "This is important." Elsa could tell that Anna understood, but she still looked disappointed.

"Don't do that," Elsa said. "You go ahead without me."

Anna hesitated. "Are you sure?"

Elsa nodded and then turned to Kai. "I'm ready," she said. "Let them in."

Moments later, a long line of people filed into the room. Anna stepped away from the throne as the villagers approached. She left the chamber quietly, following the line of people, which extended all the way through the palace courtyard into the village.

*

The first villager Kai brought before Elsa was a farmer named Niels. He grew grains and vegetables for the town.

"Good day, Your Majesty," he said, bowing deeply. "It's an honor to meet you."

"It's nice to meet you, too," Elsa said. "What brings you here?"

"Well, I heard what you did for the ice harvesters," Niels said. The other villagers in the room murmured with excitement.

"I was wondering if you could help me with my crop."

"What's the trouble with your crop?" she asked.

"Lately, we've had wonderful weather in Arendelle . . . for people," Niels explained. "But all those days of sunshine have been hard on my brussels sprouts."

"How can I help?"

"My sprouts taste much better after a thin coating of snow, Your Majesty," Niels said. "I thought you might be able to . . . you know." The farmer wiggled his fingers as if he were casting a spell.

Elsa was eager to help the villagers in any way she could. If that meant using her powers, she was happy to do it. But she couldn't just make it snow on the other side of the kingdom.

Elsa asked Kai to fetch a wagon. Then she stood and swirled her fingers through the air. She filled the wagon with a beautiful pile of fluffy snow.

"When you return home, just spread the snow around your fields," she said to Niels. "Will that help your vegetables?"

"Yes! Thank you, Your Majesty!" Niels said gratefully. "My crops will be happy for the water, too!" He bowed again before he left the chamber, happily pushing the wagon of snow.

The next villager in line was a piemaker named Tilda. She was thrilled to meet the queen, and greeted Elsa with her best curtsy. All of the villagers in the room knew Tilda and loved her pies. That was the problem.

"I make a lot of pies, Your Majesty," Tilda explained. "But I have nowhere to keep them until they're sold. I used to place them on my windowsill, but the children would stick their thumbs in them."

"I'm sorry to hear that," Elsa said sympathetically.

"I don't like to leave them out anyhow," Tilda said. "If they sit too long, my banana creams spoil and my meringues melt."

Elsa frowned, puzzled by the dilemma. She wasn't a baker, but there had to be a way to keep the pies fresh. "What about an icebox?" she suggested.

"I would love an icebox," Tilda replied. "But I can't afford one. Besides, none of the iceboxes I've seen at any of the trading posts are large enough for all my pies."

Elsa knew what to do. She summoned her frosty powers and a chill whipped through the audience chamber. Tilda shivered, but not for long. Elsa quickly conjured a huge box made entirely of ice. The box glistened in the middle of the audience chamber. It was twice as big as the icebox in the royal kitchen. "Put your pies in this," Elsa said. "That should keep them fresh. Perhaps you could even pack the icebox in straw to make it last longer."

"Oh, thank you, Your Majesty!" Tilda said. "Now I have my very own icebox."

Elsa called for servants to help Tilda carry the box. The baker left with a smile on her face.

*

By now the sun was in the middle of the sky. It was afternoon, and Elsa had spent the entire morning helping the people of Arendelle. The villagers were very nice and very grateful, but she had to admit she was growing tired.

The next villager in line was a tall blond man with a funny accent.

"Hoo, hoo! My name's Oaken," he announced. "I run a trading post. Wandering Oaken's Trading Post and Sauna, *ja?*"

"Lovely to see you again, Oaken," Elsa replied. "How can I help you today?"

First Oaken offered the queen half off on a brand-new pair of snowshoes, and then he explained his troubles. He wanted to build an ice room for his customers. That way they could cool down quickly after the sauna.

"An entire room made out of ice? Are you sure?" Elsa asked.

"*Ja!*" Oaken said enthusiastically.

Elsa agreed. The cold had never bothered her. In fact, she preferred it. She and Oaken set to work drawing up plans for the ice room. They decided that Elsa would go to the trading post to help build it the next day.

"Hoo, hoo!" Oaken said as he dashed off. Elsa smiled. She could tell that for Oaken, "hoo, hoo" meant many things. One of them was "thank you."

Elsa gazed out across the audience chamber. The line of villagers still stretched into the courtyard. Even though she had spent half the day working, it looked as though she hadn't helped anyone at all. There were just as many people waiting for her now as there had been in the morning.

Elsa sighed. It was going to be a long afternoon. Most of all, she missed Anna.

Chapter 6

Meanwhile, Anna had reluctantly gone on the picnic without her sister. She met up with her new friends on a beautiful hillside in full bloom. Lise, Thea, and Sigrid had all grown up in the village. Anna had first met them on one of her first adventures in Arendelle.

"Where's your sister?" Lise asked. "I packed lunch for five."

"She couldn't make it," Anna said. "She had some . . . queen stuff to do."

"Oh, that's too bad," Thea said. "I was looking forward to meeting her."

Sigrid spread a large patchwork blanket out on the grass. The four girls sat around Lise's picnic basket. They unpacked their lunch. The basket was full of sandwiches and delicious tarts. For dessert, Anna had brought flangendorfers.

"So, Anna, what's it like to live in the castle?" Sigrid asked. She lived on a dairy farm. Every morning she got up early and milked the cows. Then she helped her father deliver milk to the village.

"I guess it's not so different from living on a farm," Anna answered, placing a sandwich on her plate.

"Are you joking?" Thea asked. Her father was a fisherman. She spent a lot of time at sea with her brothers and sisters. "It's the castle! It's beautiful! I bet no one ever tells you to clean your room."

"That's not true," Anna laughed. "Kai tells me to clean my room all the time!"

"But you have servants!" said Lise. Her parents were merchants who traded for silk and spices.

"The servants help us take care of the palace, but we still have big responsibilities," Anna explained.

The girls chatted as they ate. The

midday sun was bright. They basked in the warm afternoon light.

"Does the castle get lonely sometimes?" Sigrid asked, curious.

Anna thought for a moment. There were times when the castle did get lonely. She thought of all those years Elsa had spent locked away from her, hiding her powers. "It can be," Anna said. "Don't get me wrong. I'm really lucky to live there. But I guess the most important thing isn't the castle; it's the people in it."

"What do you mean?" Lise asked.

Anna shrugged, searching for a way to explain. "Well, the castle's just a castle," she said. "It's my family that makes it a home."

"I think I understand," Thea said. "Without my brothers and sisters, the fishing boat wouldn't be the same."

"Yes!" Sigrid chimed in eagerly. "I can't imagine the farm without the cows!"

Lise laughed gently. "Are you sure you mean the cows, and not your family?" she asked Sigrid.

"The cows are family," Sigrid said seriously. "Besides, they never ask me to clean my room."

The four girls laughed.

*

Later, when the girls were finished eating, they stretched out on the picnic blanket. Anna, Lise, Thea, and Sigrid gazed up at the fluffy white clouds floating across the sky.

I wish Elsa were here, Anna thought.

As if reading her thoughts, Lise asked, "So, what is your sister like?"

Anna plucked a bright green blade of grass and twirled it between her fingers. "Elsa's great," she replied. "She's funny, and she's smart. And she's creative. She even made this really cool ice palace once."

The more Anna thought about Elsa, the more she missed her. She wondered how things were going back at the palace.

"It can't be easy to be the queen," Lise said. "I bet there's a lot to do."

"Tell me about it!" Anna said. "When I left this morning, there was a whole line of people waiting for Elsa to help them."

"Who helps Elsa?" Thea asked.

Anna opened her mouth to answer, but then she closed it again. It was a good question. She wasn't sure she knew the answer. There were servants at the palace who could get Elsa anything she needed, but that wasn't exactly the same. Who was there to help her laugh? Who was there to help her rest? Who was there to help pick her up when she was down?

Anna grew worried. It was *her* job to help her sister, and she wasn't there.

Suddenly, the hillside darkened. The fluffy clouds that had been dancing across the sky only moments before had vanished. In their place were gray clouds.

"Uh-oh, it looks like it's going to rain," Sigrid said.

Everyone stood and packed up the picnic. Anna had just finished helping Thea fold the blanket when a tiny snowflake floated down from the sky. Anna looked up. Yes, it was starting to

snow. She could see the flakes falling lightly on the castle.

"Does that usually happen?" Thea asked.

"Not at this time of year," Anna said, puzzled.

"Maybe it's a sign," Sigrid offered. The other girls gave her a doubtful look.

It sounded strange, but Anna wondered if Sigrid was right. Anna looked toward the castle again. Her eyes widened as she finally understood. Elsa needed her!

Chapter 7

Anna and her friends raced back to the castle. The closer they got to the castle, the heavier the snow became. When they got there, the crowd of villagers was still gathered in the courtyard. Some had pulled out umbrellas, while others held whatever they could find over their heads.

"Look at that line!" Lise exclaimed. "All those people are here to see the queen?"

"Looks that way," Anna said. She made her way through the crowd and into the castle. Her new friends followed.

In the audience chamber, Elsa was growing very tired. She'd used her powers all day, and it was finally starting to take a toll. She needed to rest and regain her strength, but she didn't want to let the people of Arendelle down.

Kai stood beside the throne. He glanced at Elsa with worried eyes.

"Maybe you should take a short break,

Your Majesty," he said gently.

"I can't, Kai," Elsa said. "The villagers are counting on me."

Even though Elsa was very tired, she did her best to smile. The next villager in line stepped forward and bowed to her.

"Your Majesty, are you okay?" he asked, concerned.

"I'm fine," she said faintly. "How can I help you?"

The villager looked doubtfully at the queen. She didn't look fine. Her face was pale, and there were dark circles under her eyes. Plus it had just started to snow *inside* the castle.

"It's okay, my queen," the villager said. "I'll come back some other time."

"No, wait—" Elsa began, but before she could finish her sentence, she collapsed. Instantly, the snow stopped and the clouds vanished.

"Elsa!" cried a voice. At the opposite end of the chamber, Anna had just arrived. She hurried over to the throne and scooped

Elsa up in her arms. Lise, Sigrid, and Thea looked on sympathetically. It definitely wasn't easy being the queen.

*

When Elsa woke the next morning, she thought she was still in the audience chamber. "How can I help you?" she murmured groggily.

Anna had been sitting patiently at her sister's bedside. When she saw that Elsa was awake, she jumped to her feet. "I'll tell you how you can help me. You can get some rest!" Anna ordered.

Elsa blinked slowly and sat up in bed. "Anna, you're here," she said softly.

"Of course I'm here," Anna replied.

"I was worried about you! When I saw the snow, I came back."

"The snow," Elsa echoed. Her features settled into anxious frown. "Is everyone okay?" She threw back the covers and tried to stand. Anna gently pushed her back against the pillows.

"Everyone's fine," Anna said. "They just thought it was an unseasonable flurry, until it starting snowing inside."

Embarrassed, Elsa covered her face with her hands. She hadn't meant for the snow to happen. Using her powers all day long had worn her out. "I just got so tired," she said.

"I know," Anna replied. "That's why you should take the day off."

"I can't. The people of Arendelle are depending on me," Elsa said. She climbed slowly to her feet. This time Anna didn't stop her. Elsa walked over to her wardrobe and pulled out a dress.

"Maybe there's a way you can help everyone without getting so tired," Anna suggested.

"I don't see how I could," Elsa said. "The villagers need me to use my powers." She thought of all the people she had helped the day before—all the wonderful things her powers had let her do. Until she'd gotten too tired, it had been fantastic.

"I get it," Anna said. "Your powers are very cool—literally! You can build palaces out of ice! You can send snowflakes whirling through the air and harvest an entire day's worth of ice in minutes. You really are a snow queen."

Elsa smiled.

"But you're also strong, and smart, and the world's best big sister," Anna added. "There are plenty of other ways for you to help the villagers. They don't need you to use your powers. Not all the time."

Elsa thought for a moment as she pulled on her dress. "But I'm good at it," she said. "I'm good at using my powers. It helps the people see that I'm not always so . . . queenly."

Elsa remembered Anna's impression of her in the square, waving stiffly to the villagers. Her sister had only been joking, but something about it rang true.

Sometimes Elsa didn't feel as close to the villagers as she wanted to. They were always so careful around her, bowing and apologizing for everything. Elsa tried her best to relate to them, but the distance was still there.

It was different for Anna. She could make a nervous young girl laugh and impress a pastry chef with a noisy belch. Elsa might have been the one with magical powers, but she didn't have Anna's people magic.

"Is that what this is about?" Anna asked. "You being queenly?"

Elsa nodded gloomily. "A little."

"Well, of course you're queenly! You're the queen! You can do anything, including helping people without using your powers!" Anna said.

Elsa's eyes brightened as she realized that Anna was absolutely right. She felt a burst of energy. She straightened her shoulders and headed for the bedroom door.

"Are you sure I can't convince you to take the day off?" Anna asked.

"And disappoint that crowd of people out there?" Elsa said, pointing to the villagers visible from her bedroom window. "No chance."

Elsa might be smart, she might be funny, and she might be the world's best big sister. But she was also stubborn. "Then I'm coming with you," Anna said, determined.

Stubbornness ran in the family.

Chapter 8

In the audience chamber, the line of villagers was just as long as it had been the day before. Elsa took her seat on the throne and greeted the people of Arendelle. Anna stood beside her.

The first villager of the day was a fish merchant named Anders. He had heard about the magic icebox Elsa had given to Tilda the piemaker. "If it's not too much trouble, would Your Majesty make one for me?" he asked. Anders needed to keep his fish cold and fresh.

Elsa thought about it for a moment. "What if I have my royal carpenters build you a large icebox out of wood or stone?" she said. "You can buy ice blocks from the harvesters and put them inside the box to keep your fish cold."

It was a perfect solution, but Anders looked disappointed. "I was hoping you would make me a box with your magic," he said hopefully.

Elsa chewed her lip as she considered it. She hated to let Anders down. It would be so easy to use her powers, and it would make him happy. "Of course I can make you a box. It's no trouble at all," she said.

Elsa wove her hands through the air in a swirl of ice crystals. Anders and the villagers waiting in line gasped in awe. With a blast of frost and a whirl of icicles, Elsa built the box.

Anders thanked her wholeheartedly. Elsa called for servants to help him carry the icebox. The fish merchant left happy.

Elsa turned to the next villager, but not before Anna tugged on her sleeve.

"You didn't have to use your powers," Anna whispered.

"I know, but he really wanted me to," Elsa replied.

"Just don't overdo it," Anna said. "Remember, there are other ways to help people."

Elsa agreed and promised Anna that she'd be careful.

*

Morning slipped by quickly again, and before long, afternoon had arrived. Even though Elsa's plan had been to help the villagers without using her powers, it was harder than she'd thought it would be. She'd given in many times, to the delight of the villagers. But Elsa was starting to feel uneasy about it. Magic was just one

part of her, and if magic was all the people expected, they would never truly know her.

A seamstress named Dagmar curtsied in front of Elsa. She explained that she ran the village laundry. "Lately, there have been more and more dirty clothes, Your Majesty, and I can't get enough water to clean them," Dagmar said.

"I'm sorry to hear that," Elsa replied sympathetically. "How can I help?"

Dagmar and the laundry workers had to carry buckets of water back and forth. There was so much laundry, they couldn't carry the water fast enough. "Is there any way your magic could help with the water, Your Majesty?" she asked.

Elsa considered Dagmar's request. The seamstress seemed to be hoping for Elsa come up with some magical solution, but Elsa knew a different way. She glanced over at Anna and remembered her words. There were other ways to help the people of Arendelle. Elsa had more than her magic to offer.

"Wait here," she said.

Elsa stepped down from the throne and left the chamber. She raced through the palace to her study.

On the desk, her plans for Arendelle's new plumbing system were right where she'd left them two days before. She scooped up the papers and ran back to the audience room.

Elsa showed the plans to Dagmar. "The pipes and canals will carry water all across the village," she said. "We can run a pipe out to you and build a water pump. You'll be able to draw water right at the laundry."

Dagmar's eyes widened in excitement as she looked at the plans. "Do you think you can do this?" she asked hopefully.

"*We* can do this," Elsa replied. She turned to address the crowd gathered in the audience chamber. "This plumbing system will benefit everyone—farmers, fisherman, and piemakers alike. If everyone pitches in, we can build the water pump in a day! Who will help me?"

The villagers murmured to each other. Digging canals and laying pipes wasn't quite as fun as watching Elsa use her magic.

"I'll help!" Anna said, stepping forward. She took Elsa's hand and squeezed it in support.

"Me too!" Dagmar said.

"I'll help!" cried a farmer.

"Count me in!" said several merchants.

Word spread along the line of villagers to the crowd in the courtyard. One by one, the people of Arendelle agreed to lend a hand.

Chapter 9

The next day, Elsa, Anna and the villagers rose early. They set out at dawn with the palace builders, plumbers, and architects. All over town, the work began. The people of Arendelle dug canals and trenches for the new plumbing system.

Kristoff and the ice harvesters were the

first to break ground. Shoveling wasn't so different from ice carving. They worked together in a well-organized team, singing the songs of the frozen lake.

Even Olaf was given a special task. He helped Chef Florian serve refreshments to the hardworking villagers. Florian was also famous for his frosty lemonade.

"Fresh-squeezed lemonade!" Olaf cried, carrying a small tray of glasses.

"Is it cold?" asked a villager, wiping the sweat from his brow.

"Of course it's cold!" Olaf replied. "Thanks to my cousins!"

By early evening, the canals were finished and most of the pipes had been laid. At Dagmar's laundry, Elsa and Anna worked side by side. The sisters were up to their elbows in dirt, putting the finishing touches on a brand-new water pump.

Anna looked at Elsa and broke into a fit of giggles.

"What's so funny?" Elsa asked.

"You don't look so queenly now," Anna said. The hem of Elsa's dress was stained

with mud, there was dirt smeared across her cheek, and her brow was drenched with sweat.

"I look absolutely queenly," Elsa said. She lifted her chin defiantly. "This is what a queen looks like when she's working."

Anna straightened up and stretched. They'd spent most of the day hunched over, digging trenches.

Elsa paused and blew a sweaty lock of hair from her eyes. "You were right, Anna," she said. "I love using my magic to help people. But some days, helping them this way is even better."

"Way to win their hearts," Anna said, smiling.

Elsa slid the pump handle into place

and called to Dagmar. The seamstress put down her shovel and hurried over to the queen.

"Why don't you give it a try," Elsa told Dagmar.

"Yeah," Anna said. "Let's see if this thing we built actually works."

Dagmar gripped the handle and lifted it up, then pushed it down. A strange gurgling noise rumbled through the pipes. Dagmar took that as a sign of encouragement and pumped faster. Suddenly, water spilled from the spout. It was cold and clear and fresh.

Dagmar was thrilled. She turned to Elsa with tears of joy in her eyes. "I don't know how to thank you!" she cried.

"I do," Anna said. "Three cheers for Queen Elsa!"

A cheer went up among the villagers. They gathered around and lifted Elsa up onto their shoulders.

"All hail the Queen!" the people of Arendelle shouted.

Chapter 10

$\mathfrak{A}$ few days later, Elsa got up, dressed, and made her way to the audience chamber. The people of Arendelle were enjoying their new water system. That particular problem had been solved, but they still came to Elsa for guidance, and she enjoyed helping them. The difference was that they didn't expect her to use her powers. Now they knew her better.

Elsa opened the doors to the audience chamber and was surprised to find it empty. Just then, Anna walked up beside her.

"I hope you don't mind, but I gave the villagers the day off," Anna said with a grin.

"The villagers don't need a day off," Elsa replied.

"But you do," she said.

"Anna, we've been over this. You know I have responsibilities. The people of Arendelle are depending on me," Elsa explained.

"I know. That's why Kai and I have

worked out a schedule. The people of Arendelle will visit the palace three days a week. The other days are for your other duties, like spending time with your sister," Anna said.

Elsa started to protest but realized there was no reason to. It was a brilliant idea. It gave her time to do everything she wanted, especially spend time with Anna. That was the hardest part about those long hours in the audience chamber—it was time spent away from her sister.

"So what's next on the list?" Elsa asked.

"You mean this list?" Anna said, pulling the scroll from her pocket. She unrolled her list of Things to Do in Arendelle. "We're up to number six."

"Let me guess, more flangendorfers," Elsa joked.

"Heavens, no!" Anna said dramatically. "Number six is going to be our biggest adventure yet."

Elsa raised an eyebrow. "What's that?" she asked doubtfully.

"Sisterly bonding," Anna said.

"Piece of cake," Elsa told her.

The two sisters clasped hands and strolled through the halls of the palace. They walked out into the courtyard, ready for their next adventure . . . together.